MOBY SHINOBI

NINJA ON THE JOB

by Luke Flowers

SCHOLASTIC INC.

FOR MY MOM AND DAD —
WHO BUILT A STRONG FOUNDATION OF ENCOURAGEMENT THROUGHOUT MY LIFE THAT HELPED ME HONE MY CREATIVE NINJA SKILLS. I AM FOREVER GRATEFUL FOR THE GIFT OF GROWING UP IN A HOME FILLED WITH HEARTY LAUGHTER, WACKY CREATIVITY, AND A BOUNTY OF LOVE.

Library of Congress Cataloging-in-Publication Data

Names: Flowers, Luke, author, illustrator. | Flowers, Luke. Moby Shinobi.
Title: Ninja on the job / by Luke Flowers.
Description: New York, NY : Scholastic Inc., 2019. | Series: Moby Shinobi |
Summary: Told in rhyme, Moby Shinobi tries to help out the construction workers building a house, but as usual his ninja skills just create chaos—until he saves a puppy that has gotten stuck in wet concrete.
Identifiers: LCCN 2018033243| ISBN 9781338256147 (pbk.) | ISBN 9781338256154 (hardcover)
Subjects: LCSH: Ninja—Juvenile fiction. | Helping behavior—Juvenile fiction. | House construction—Juvenile fiction. | Construction workers—Juvenile fiction. | Stories in rhyme. | CYAC: Stories in rhyme. | Ninja—Fiction. | Helpfulness—Fiction. | House construction—Fiction. | Construction workers—Fiction. | LCGFT: Stories in rhyme. | Humorous fiction. Classification: LCC PZ8.3.F672 Nk 2019 | DDC [E]—dc23 LC record available at https://lccn.loc.gov/2018033243

10 9 8 7 6 5 4 3 2   19 20 21 22 23

Printed in the U.S.A.   40
First printing 2019
Book design by Steve Ponzo

3

6

8

Moby thinks of a ninja chop!
He puts a piece of wood on top.

AHHH! These broken boards will NOT do! Let's find a different job for you.

12

13

**Moby thinks of a fast attack.
He prepares for a double whack!**

SNAP!

SMASH!

20

Moby thinks of his ninja cart.
He knows just where he needs to start!

24

25

27

28

Moby thinks of a giant climb.
He knows he does not have much time!